ZIP

The story of a carrier pigeon in WWII

Story by Diane Condon-Boutier

Illustrations by Elisabeth Gontier

Zip : The Story of a Carrier Pigeon in WWII

In memory of my Uncle Joe, who first told me that my pig-headed, stubborn refusal to give up learning to water ski could be called perseverance, but only once I stayed up for over ten seconds...

My name is Zip. I am a pigeon, but not just any sort of pigeon. I am a carrier pigeon. I am a carrier pigeon who helped the Allied Special Operations during WW2. I guess you could call me a spy pigeon.

Wonder how this all came about? Sometimes I do too!

I hatched on a farm in England with lots of other pigeons. It's like having a really big family. Several fowl keepers take care of us: feeding us, cleaning our nesting boxes and teaching us a routine of going outside in the mornings and flying back to roost in the early evening.

Until one day, a whole slew of important looking people moved into the manor house on our farm, called Bletchley Park, and things began to change. Men and women in uniforms - and some in smart looking civilian clothes -come and go,

carrying typewriters and boxes of papers. Radio equipment is set up and large antennas are installed, hidden high in the trees. Cars, lorries and bicycles come and go every day. Everyone looks very busy.

By listening to conversations among our keepers we learned that all this activity is because England is at war. We became part of an Alliance of nations, standing together against the tyranny of Nazi Germany.

To me, the Nazi regime sounds like a terrible thing. The basic principles of freedom and democracy which govern the countries making up the Alliance are crushed in  Germany, and in the whole of the European continent which the Nazi army has invaded and occupied. We hear frightening stories of the Nazi ruler, Adolph Hitler, and what a horrible person he is.

We, as English, feel rather lucky to be on an island separated from the continent by the English Channel. It gives us a small natural barrier, which the Nazis attempted to break during the first few years of the war. They flew over our English cities and dropped hundreds of thousands of bombs. This period was known as the Blitz, or the Battle of Britain.

Even though the German airplanes making up the Luftwaffe, or German Air Force, zoomed over in waves of dozens at a time, my flying friends in the Royal Air Force certainly showed them some fancy aviation tricks. I was terribly impressed. And as you might guess, flying is my thing.

Generally, birds and airplanes try to stay away from each other. I have seen too many accidents to forget that crossing paths with a B-24 Liberator in my airspace is a serious mistake. A B-24, although they're pretty smart machines flown by brave and gifted men, cannot swerve out of the way of a flock of birds. That's no good for either party involved. So, I prefer to observe from a safe distance, thank you very much!

Still, our airplanes and pilots serve an important purpose in attacking the enemy, intercepting their planes and blasting them out of the sky before they can drop bombs, harming innocent civilians.

At first, my job wasn't clear to me. Watching those airplanes, I thought I might be taught to carry tiny bombs over specific targets. I rather hoped to be able to swoop down and destroy something in a spectacular dive. I practiced my swooping and diving  and veering left and right, hoping to attract the attention of my caretakers. You see, if they noticed how swift and daring I was, they might suggest that I be picked for Special Operations training.

My neighbor, lodging a few crates down from mine, is older than myself, having hatched a full year before I did. His name is Horatio. I thought that was quite an exotic name for a pigeon until I found out that it was chosen for him because of the serial letters and numbers attached to a small band around his leg. The series begins with an H, followed by several numbers before ending with an O. Thus, the name chosen for him.

I'll never forget him watching as my mother encouraged me to take off for the first time and I crash landed in the yard. He didn't make fun of me, although most of the other pigeons fell over in their cages, they were laughing so hard. Of course, I was embarrassed but determined to get it right, so I tried again and again...and again.

He cheered when I finally got airborne, and later, when I was moved to my own crate, he took me under his wing and gave me a few pointers.

As a young bird, I spent a lot of energy showing off my talents whenever the men wearing uniforms loaded with medals came to speak with our caretakers.

Each time, I watched sadly as the older, stronger pigeons with a larger wingspan than my own were singled out and taken away. It wasn't clear where they were going, but those of us left behind spoke about it each time a new group left, wondering why we were still here and why our friends never seemed to return.

It was very frustrating. But I continued to practice every day, and soon I was flying higher and longer, and farther and faster than I ever had. Horatio kept after me every day. "Turn your stubbornness into perseverance! Make it work for you and not against you!" he would say, although I wasn't sure what he meant.

Until yesterday, a pigeon who had been driven off in a lorry came back to his old roost. He flew in and collapsed in the yard, out of breath. His chest was heaving and his eyes rolling like he was about to die.

He lived in the crate next door to Horatio, and he'd taught me a lot about diving into air currents to rest during long flights. Shortly after his tumbled landing, one of our care-takers let out a whoop of joy and began rushing around the yard shouting for the other caretakers to join him. Our exhausted friend was scooped up and carried away.

So many questions jostled about in my head! Where had he been? What had he seen? What was his mission? Did he encounter any difficulties? Exactly what is it that we're expected to do?

Horatio said, "You see Zip, that pigeon continued on until he made it home. That's perseverance."

I wish I knew what that other pigeon had been through. I wish I could ask him all the questions flitting through my head like a swarm of bugs on a summer afternoon. Until then, my curiosity would be killing me! In the meantime, I've got practice to do.

My job gets a little harder every week. I'm taken out of my box. One of the keepers straps a small tube on my leg, and then I'm placed in the back of a lorry with some of my friends. They drive us away from our yard, every day in a different direction and every day farther than the last.

Today, when our caretakers stop the vehicle and begin to unload us, they fill the tubes on our legs with pebbles. This adds weight to one side. Noticing something on the ground resembling a plump, tasty insect, I hop down and immediately fall over. Frantic flapping of my wings sets me upright once again. But as soon as I attempt to walk, I veer off to one side dragging the foot with the tube on it.

One of our caretakers has noticed my problem. "Harry! How many pebbles did you put in Zip's tube? The poor bird can't even walk!" He catches me and removes about half of the contents of the tube before attaching it firmly to my leg once again. I take a few awkward steps, waddling in a way which makes me feel as if I've made myself sick by overeating.

In the meantime, the bug has disappeared. So much for my tempting snack! As I scan the ground for another, I'm called to attention by Horatio.

"Zip! Stop thinking about your stomach and get off the ground!" Horatio zooms by in a dramatic swoop just over-head as he shouts at me. "Come on! You'll never get chosen if you can't do the job!"

"Hah! Gotcha!" The bug, that is. As I waddle away, picking up speed, I spy it under a leaf on the path. Skidding to a halt, I pluck the bug off the ground, spit out the leaf and begin to run while gulping and flapping my wings. I'm off! Snack swallowed and ready to catch up with the others heading home!

Flying is an incredible feeling. Currents of air skim my wings, supporting the added weight in the red tube attached to my leg. I feel the need to flap a little harder and a bit more often than usual, but I'm strong enough to support the extra weight with no problem at all. My pre-flight snack helped! All the way home we chatter among ourselves, racing each other, swerving in near a friend to share a word and pass the time. Flying in a group is great fun.

Still, today's flight is a long one and while at first, I thought the extra weight wouldn't be a problem, I'm beginning to tire.

"Horatio, I need a break!" I spot a tree ahead with a nice open spot in the leaves, tempting me to slip in and rest awhile.

"Perseverance, Zip! Keep at it!"

"No, I'm tired, I need a break."

"Are you sure you can't make it? You really shouldn't eat before a long flight, you'll get cramp. You've been told that over and over. You probably didn't even look to see what kind of a bug was. Maybe it was an inedible one!" Horatio shakes his head. "I don't know why you eat bugs anyway, we've got a plentiful supply of grain. It's good for us, we digest it easily. But no! you've got to dig up wild things instead!"

"I'm just tired. I need to stop for a rest. I'll catch up."

"No, no. I'm not leaving you here alone. You might get into trouble. I'll stop too." Horatio grumbles, but follows me into the shady greenery of the treetop. The branch I choose is wide and an easy roosting spot for two.

"Pfooof! I'm bushed!" Standing on one leg I stretch the cartouche carrying leg out to one side and shake it. The pebbles rattle inside.

"It's not even full! You know, during the last war, there were pigeons not any bigger than you are today, who carried cameras into battle to take photographs of the enemy positions. They helped our officers decide what moves to make. Their work saved many soldiers' lives! You can't even carry a full tube of pebbles!"

"I'm doing my best..." I'm feeling pretty bad about not keeping up with the others and Horatio sees he's hurt my feelings.

"I'm telling you this for your own good. You want to be chosen to fly missions, right? So, stop with the bug and berry eating and instead eat your grain. It builds muscle and you'll grow stronger quickly."

"But, I love bugs and berries!"

"Well, if you love them more than flying, then go right ahead and eat up. If you're serious about the work we're trained to do, eat your grain and leave the bugs and berries to the sparrows. It's all about perseverance!"

Just then, a ladybug lands right next to me. As I reach my beak down to snatch it, Horatio shouts "Watch out!"

Something crashes through the leaves, breaking twigs and sending the ladybug hurtling off into space. I lose my balance as Horatio takes off through the branches, bursting into flight.

I shake myself into action just as another rock flies by, grazing my left wing. There's a little boy on one of the lower branches with a slingshot! He's trying to knock me out!

16

"Drat it all! I missed!" shouts the boy to another boy standing beneath the tree. "We could have had roast pigeon for supper tonight! Mum would have been so pleased!"

What a horrible thing to say! Those boys actually want to cook me up for supper!

"Horatio! Wait up!" My wing stings a bit, but I'm flapping in a panic to catch up to him and get out of the range of further rock slinging.

"Did you hear that? Those kids wanted to eat us!"

"Yes, well not all humans are as friendly to birds as our keepers. What do you think happens to pigeons who don't do their job?"

"What? You mean that if I don't do my job, I'll be eaten by someone?" I simply cannot believe this news.

"Zip, let's just get back to roost, ok?"

"But Horatio! You've got to tell me the truth!"

"Not now! Fly!" He speeds off ahead and I get flapping even harder, wondering what ladybugs taste like.

We reach the yard shortly after the others. The keepers are still serving scoops of grain as we swoop into our open crates. Still thinking about what I've learned about humans and their taste for pigeon, I'm hoping my caretakers won't notice our tardy arrival. A scoop of grain and a splash of water are provided by human hands I was never afraid of before. Now, I step to the back of the box, until they close the latch on the door. I stretch out my sore wing and my handler notices. He reaches in and closes his hands around my body. For the first time ever, I struggle.

"Hey, birdie, calm down. I won't hurt you."

I can't keep from thinking: 'That's what you say now, but I'll bet you like eating pigeon paté!'

He gently smooths the one feather on top of my head which never lays down flat. Then, he smooths the feathers along my grazed shoulder, stretches the wing out, sees the nicked spot, and lets my wing return to a folded position.

"Had a run in with something did you, Zip?" He rubs two fingers along my shoulders in a neck massage. I cannot help but close my eyes in bliss. The flight was long and my shoulder muscles are tired. Having the keeper rub them feels wonderful. "Well, you'll be just fine with a day off to-morrow. You rest up and stay around close, where you'll be safe from any local kids with slingshots." He puts me gently back into my nesting box. "In you go, eat up and rest and you'll be as good as new in no time!" The latch slips into place and I'm safe inside for the night.

****

Later that evening, I wake to sounds of my fellow pigeons rustling about and flapping their wings inside their crates. Usually, this means there's some sort of danger. I peer through the wire in my door to see what's going on.

It's Joseph, our friend who crash landed in the yard after being gone for so long. He's been returned to his old nesting box.

I hear Horatio whispering to him.

"Hey, Joseph! Glad to see you back, mate! Where've you been? Any news to share?"

"You can't imagine how glad I am to be back, Horatio! I never thought I'd make it." Joseph wagged his head from side to side. "You have no idea what it's like out there! I hope I am never given another mission. I almost died a dozen times!"

A collective gasp and much flapping of wings could be heard from the group of pigeons listening in to this exciting conversation.

"So, tell us already! We're dying of curiosity!"

"Is it true that if we don't do missions, we'll be turned into pie for the officers' supper?" I can't help blurting out the question that's been bothering me since this afternoon's run in with those sling-shot wielding boys.

"Shut up, kid and let him talk!"

Joseph's kind voice reaches me over someone else's rude remark.

"Hey, kiddo! So, you've grown up enough to move over here with the big guys, hey? Good for you. Your ma must be proud."

"Yes, sir, Mister Joseph. I hope she is and I'd like to make her even prouder by doing my bit to end this war. Can you tell us what you did?"

"Yes, yes, tell us!"

"Share your story!"

"Shut up, kid!"

"Let Joseph tell his story!"

"Please Joseph! Tell us everything!"

So many voices! So much noise!

"Settle down or we won't hear a thing!" Horatio's voice carries through the general excitement, calming every voice and commanding silence.

"Well, it's like this, you might remember the day I was taken away? Well I was driven to an airfield and they loaded my crate and almost a dozen other pigeons - some of them I didn't even know- directly onto an airplane! I was going to take off and fly, but not by my own wing-power! It was incredibly noisy and bumpy! Let me just say that an airplane take-off is nowhere near as easy or smooth as it is for us..."

Joseph's voice carried on long into the night, telling his incredible story and we listened, hanging on every word. Before we knew it, sparrows and finches were twittering about in the high branches beginning their dawn chorus.

"...and just when I thought I couldn't flap a single time more, I saw the roof of the big house and I knew I was home. I swear I wanted to cry after all I'd been through. You saw me crash into the yard, but it didn't even hurt. I was just so happy to be here."

We were, all of us, stunned into silence. Could it be true? We had been trained to carry messages in our leg tubes? Maps? Information so important that it didn't matter if we survived our flight? That the German soldiers tried to shoot at us with their guns? To kill us and take the information we carried? And that even the people we were carrying messages to might decide to kill us for food? Or because they were afraid to be caught with us? And that in addition to birds of prey: the hawks and owls which we always have to be afraid of, there's an entire army of soldiers out to kill us?

All these questions and the terrifying answers to them provided by Joseph needed time to be discussed.

Yet, there's no time at all because it's already morning and our handlers are transferring us into barrel shaped travel cages. These are made of wood and have a door on the front with a grate for us to look out.

"Wait! Not me! I have a nicked shoulder, remember? I'm supposed to have a day off to get better!" I rustle around inside and stretch my wing out, to show the man picking up my barrel that I have a wound, but he's not paying any attention.

"Hey Bill, how many have you loaded? I've got six here."

"Me too. That makes an even dozen! Off we go guys! We've got work to do, birdies!"

Someone forgot to tell these two men that I am supposed to have a day off. Evidently, I'll just have to go right ahead and be strong. Perseverance! But I get to thinking as I stretch my wing, trying to warm up my sore muscles. What if today is the day it's my turn to go? I thought I was ready. I thought I was brave. But this long night, listening to Joseph makes me sure I am neither brave, nor ready.

It's a lot to think about as we drive along the bumpy road toward today's drop off point. It seems to take forever, so I close one eye and try to rest, but cannot.

****

No pebbles in my tube today. Instead they put in a piece of paper. I have no idea what it is but I realize that today's flight is going to be a lot easier with a paper in my tube instead of rocks. Good, because my shoulder's still quite sore.

A long drive takes us to a large field with lots of activity. Vehicles are driving in every direction. Our truck swerves out of the way of a jeep carrying important looking, uniformed men. They climb out and approach our truck.

"Are these the birds?"

"Yes, sir."

A finger pokes between the wire grid on the door of my barrel. I'm tempted to peck at it, just because who wants to be poked at? Still, I assume this finger must belong to someone important who wouldn't appreciate being pecked, whether he deserves it or not. I keep remembering the threat of pigeon pie.

In the near distance, I hear an airplane engine start. Good grief, they're letting us loose near an airfield? How silly of them! Everybody knows birds and planes don't mix! Are they testing us to see who's smart enough to stay away from airplanes?

Two men pick up my barrel. They roll it around and I scramble to stay on my feet but fall over as they jostle it from side to side, attaching something to it.

"So, how does this work?"

"Well sir, the parachute deploys by pulling on this cord. The birds will be dropped from about 400 feet once we've located the area indicated by the French Resistance."

"We're dropping a dozen birds with maps of the general area. They'll each have a small, loosely woven, linen bag with grain in it, which they can actually peck apart to feed themselves in case it takes a day or two for someone to find them. When that happens, we can only hope it will be someone willing to put an "X" on the map where the V1 missile launch site is located and set the bird free. He'll then fly back to Bletchley and we'll have our information for planning a bombing raid on that site."

"These birds can fly that far? It's several hundred miles. How do you know? Have they flown such a distance be-fore?"

"No Sir, the farthest training mission has been about 50 miles, but they've consistently returned home, so we believe they can do this. And if we're wrong, well, we won't be out much for trying."

I am dumbstruck.

It's today.

I'm going on my very first mission today!

26

****

The pigeons in the barrel cages next to me seem to be just as surprised as I am.

"What's a V1 anyway?" one of them asks.

"I don't know, but I've heard them called doodlebugs."

"Wait...what? They're hoping to bomb a bug's nest? What for?" my neighbor asks.

I realize that I'm clearly not as silly as some pigeons, so I kindly explain, "Errr, I think that might be a nickname for something much bigger. Certainly, a dangerous Nazi missile launch site. They're not sending airplanes to bomb bugs."

"Oh, yeah. You're probably right. I wonder what it looks like though..."

"Let's just keep listening to our handlers and the airmen and we might find out."

"Good idea!"

It's not long before we see the pilot and another man approaching a small airplane. Following close behind is a girl. She's zipping up her jumpsuit and putting on flight goggles. What's all this about? Why is there a girl coming along?

Our truck is maneuvered closer to the plane whose propeller is whirling and whipping up a lot of dust and wind. It's almost impossible to hear anything at all over the roar of the engine.

The girl comes over to look at us. "Awww, are these the birds?" She pokes a finger through the wire grid. Why do humans do that? It's very annoying! Still, she seems nice enough so I don't fuss about it. "You poor birdies! You've got no idea, have you?" She pulls her finger out, turns and walks away.

Just what did that mean? Poor birdies? Now I'm really starting to get worried!

Our truck stops alongside the plane whose engine is humming. The wind and noise are quite scary. The girl climbs in a small door on the side of the plane. The men driving our truck get out. One of them opens my door and tosses a woven cloth bag inside. I know what this is, and right now I could care less about food. He picks up my barrel and slides it in the side door and the girl pushes me across the floor inside of the plane. The other barrels slide in beside mine. The men give the girl a jaunty wave before shutting the door and locking us in darkness.

Before we can even discuss what's happening the plane begins to rumble down the airstrip, vibrating, shaking and making more noise than I've ever heard. Suddenly, I feel us lift off the ground and the shaking stops. I'm airborne! And for first time in my life I'm not doing the flying. I'm not sure I like it.

After a few hours of nothing happening at all, I realize that this kind of flying is actually quite boring. I can't see anything, I don't feel the wind in my feathers and I don't feel the thrill of gliding or swooping. I even take a nap for a while. I wake up when I feel us slowing down and losing altitude. It's very dark in here, but I can hear someone moving around nearby.

Suddenly a trap door is opened in the floor near my barrel and I can see outside. It's night, but there's a lovely full moon shining down, almost smiling at us. One of the pilots and the girl are moving among the crates, checking the ropes attached to the tops.

"Ok, these look alright, and yours?" he shouts at her.

"Just dandy! Ready? Cause there's the coast of Dieppe right there! Just a few minutes south and we'll be over Bacque- ville."

"Look for the church! And when you see it, push out your kegs and pull the handles!"

"Ok, got 'em!" she shouts.

"Now!"

And out I go, falling inside my barrel! In- stinctively, I try to flap my wings. It doesn't help!

But, just as quickly I feel a big jerk and now I'm floating: still dropping from the sky, but much slower.

The graceful floating ends with a brutal crash and tumble. My barrel rolls and I'm rolling inside of it, bumping off the walls. Another thud stops the barrel although I'm still rolling around inside, trying to find my feet. For a minute, my eyes feel like they've rolled someplace off my head. So, I shake all over, ruffling my feathers and flapping my wings just to settle everything back in place.

I'm looking out into darkness, across the silvery paving of a moonlit courtyard, when I hear the heavy chested voice of a very large dog. It lets out a series of deep and threatening 'woof!' barks, one at a time, as if expecting an answer it's not getting.

I'm wishing I spoke large dog language. In general, large dogs and birds don't get along very well, so I'm wishing I could let this one know that I'm a friend and that I come in peace.

The barking is coming from a cottage across the courtyard. A door cracks, letting out a sliver of light and a gigantic Saint Bernard hurls itself in a loping gallop across the paving, aiming straight at me!

I flap frantically trying to lift off the ground but of course I can't, because I'm trapped inside this barrel and no amount of flapping will get both me and my barrel into the air.

I'm doomed and my entire life flashes before my eyes. Since I'm very young, it doesn't take long. I open one eye just as an enormous, snorting, wet, dog nose shoves into the wire mesh of my door. A huge, hairy head blocks out any light and hot, rather smelly breath blows in great puffs into my face.

This is unacceptable and I must let this dog know it. "Hey, knock it off, will ya? Your breath smells like you've been eating cow manure!"

"Grrrrouuuuufff!" it answers.

"Oh yeah? Well you too!" This animal's not very polite, so I'm not going to be either!

"Polka! Be quiet, girl! Come here!" says a man's voice from somewhere behind the shaggy, snorting, dog head.

"Wow! You're a girl? I'd never have guessed! And you should brush up on your manners, too!" If I'm going to be eaten by this dog, I'm going to give her a piece of my mind beforehand!

"*Alors,* what have we got here?" says the voice, while hands reach down to pick up the barrel. "Quick, Polka! Let's get back inside! *Allez, viens, ma fille!*"

The old man hurries across the courtyard and all three of us enter the cottage. He places my barrel on the stone floor in front of a fireplace, warm and crackling with a cheerful fire, then locks the door.

The dog is back, snuffling and pushing the barrel with her nose. I'm not enjoying all this rough and tumble action and let out several shrill squawks. The dog barks again. The man scolds her.

"Polka! You must be quiet or you'll alert the Germans! *Tais-toi!*"

Oh no! I get it now! This is occupied France! That's why this old man is speaking French! We flew across the English Channel in the airplane while I was sleeping! This is getting worse and worse.

The old man clips off each of the cords attaching the parachute to the keg and rolls the cord into little balls which he places in a drawer. Next, he spreads the parachute out on a table and carefully folds it into a neat square, before putting it in an armoire.

"Polka, go lay down. Off to your bed, *ma fille!*" The dog very obediently goes to collapse onto a blanket, folded into a large enough rectangle to serve as her bed, but keeps her eyes glued to me.

"Now, let's have a closer look." The old man sits on a bench close to the light of the fire and opens the latch on my barrel just a crack. I make a dash for freedom. But, his hands are quick to catch me as I try to burst through the door. "Woah, woah, woah! *Arrete!* Old Emile won't hurt you, little bird!"

I cannot resist giving him a peck on the knuckle.

"*Aie!* Don't bite old Emile, you silly thing! I said I won't hurt you!"

Everything I've seen and heard lately makes me doubt his words. Recently, I narrowly escaped being caught and eaten by little boys wishing to bring me home and cook me for their dinner. I've been told that pigeons who don't do their jobs end up as *paté* for the British officers' lunch and that the entire German army shoots pigeons just for fun. Humans aren't well positioned on my list of friends right now. Even though this one seems nice enough, his huge dog is staring at me as if she'd rather swallow me than become friends.

This is certainly not a good day to be a pigeon. Even worse, I'm a pigeon who's far from home and I have a sore shoulder. Now that I think about it, I want to cry. I begin to shiver, and before I can help it, small squeaking noises begin coming out of my beak.

"*Oh, voilà!* Just look, Polka, we've scared this young pigeon! And him so brave to be tossed off a plane into our yard! I wonder what he's carrying in his message tube. Let's have a look, shall we?"

Emile holds me tight against his chest with his left hand, and gently opens the top of the bright red cartouche attached to my leg. He slips one finger inside and slides out a tiny roll of paper. Once he places this on the bench next to him, he continues to hold me close, speaking softly and stroking my feathers.

This has a calming effect on me and I relax against his chest, enjoying feeling warm and quiet. When he begins to rub my neck between his thumb and index, I close my eyes in bliss. Maybe he won't hurt me. Maybe he doesn't think paté made of carrier pigeon is tasty at all. Maybe he won't feed me to his dog. Maybe I can live here in France with him. Maybe I could learn enough French to get along just fine. Maybe I'll take a nap.

When I wake up, I smell something strange.

Woah! I'm back inside my barrel, sitting on the table with the door open and the dog is looking at me. Very closely! Her breath is what I'm smelling. I don't know what Emile feeds her, but she should try some of my grain.

Hey! That reminds me. I'm hungry! Where's that cloth bag?

Oh no! Emile must have done this! It's outside my barrel, sitting on the table very close to the dog's head. The dog must be reading my mind because she turns to look at it. Just as I poke my head out to take a step towards the bag, the monster picks it up with her slobbery mouth! She's carrying it away!

36

Hey! No! That's mine! I rush out of the barrel and run across the table as she makes off with my bag of grain, trots over to her bed and drops it.

No way, Madame! You are not having my breakfast! I take wing and swoop down at her, squawking as if my life depended on it. Emile looks up, surprised. I hadn't noticed him dozing in an armchair by the fire. He drops the paper in his hand as he jumps up.

"Stop!" I squawk. The dog sits down on my bag of grain and barks at me as I fly around the room, veering in circles near her head. Emile grabs a newspaper and begins to flap it at me, making me even angrier.

This is just too much! First the dog steals my food, now Emile is swatting at me like I'm a wasp! I can see only one thing to do in such a situation. I swoop low over the dog and relieve myself.

Yes, that's it. I've pooped on the dog.

Polka stops barking immediately, looking shocked. Emile drops his newspaper and bursts out laughing as I land on the table and take refuge in my barrel, feeling satisfied. I've effectively expressed my opinion about the dog and this entire situation. I'm still hungry, but my stomach will just have to wait.

"Well old girl, I guess that pigeon showed you, didn't he?" Emile is still chuckling as he opens the door and shoos the dog outside. I can see that it's gently raining. "Polka, how about you spend some time out there and get rinsed off a bit?"

****

Emile brings the rolled paper to the table near my barrel where I'm happily pecking at the grain he's set out in a little dish. I'm also enjoying a small glass of cool water he's given me. I was right, he's a kind man. Polka is sitting outside in the rain with her head on the window sill, look-ing in at us with lolling tongue and forlorn, drooping eyes. I'm enjoying myself greatly.

Even I should know that this can't last.

"So, you've brought me a map, young bird. I wonder if you know what this is? Well, since we're friends now, I'll tell you." Emile stretches out his hand to stroke the stand-up feather on my head as I peck at the grain which today, ex-ceptionally, I find delicious.

"You have a special map. One that shows the place I live and the villages nearby. On the top are words written in a very old form of French. They say *'Honni soit qui mal y pense!'* In today's language that means 'Shame on he of bad designs!' I remember that motto from a book I read as a young boy about the Knights of the Order of the Garter. I think whoever wrote this wants me to know that they're honorable people who want to help the French rid ourselves of the dishonorable Nazis. What do you think?"

If only I could make him understand what I thought! If I could speak in Emile's language, or he, in mine, I could tell him that I come from England, from a place where hundreds of men, women and pigeons are working hard every day to make the dream of freedom for all of Europe come true. I remember what the uniformed men at home said the map was for. I look him straight in the eyes, tilting my head, hoping he can read this thought in my mind and in my heart: 'Emile, you must mark an X on the site of the V1 missile launch site nearby, and I will take the map back to England.'

I think this thought over and over again, trying to make him understand. I keep looking him in the eye and thinking the same thought as hard as I can. He looks closely at my eyes and I believe he understands.

Emile sighs heavily as he rises from the bench, turning his back on me. "If I do what I think this map wants me to do, it will bring swarms of Allied airplanes here, to my home. They will drop bombs all over the place, trying to destroy that terrible Nazi missile launch site. Some of those bombs might miss their target. They might fall on the homes of my friends and neighbors. I will be responsible for the damage they cause, if I put an X on your map."

I think the thought again: 'Emile, you must mark an X on the site of the V1 missile launch site nearby, and I will take the map back to England.'

Emile looks in my eyes again, as I tilt my head, thinking the thought over and over, hoping to make him understand.

"But, if I don't put an X on the spot, then the Nazis will continue to fire their deadly missiles at England, trying to kill innocent women and children. You know, little bird, it's not just English civilians who die from their missiles. One of the last ones they  fired from the launch site hidden at the farm down the road from here landed in the center of Auppegard. That's just a mile away. When it crashed, a crowd of villagers came out to look at it, wondering what it was. Then, it exploded, killing innocent French men, women and children. Many died, many were wounded. Yes, I think someone must stop that from happening again. And yet, I am afraid to put my neighbors in danger. What should I do?"

I think the thought again. Over and over, concentrating just on that one thought, willing him to help me complete my mission.

Emile paces the room. He too, is thinking hard.

Finally, he picks up a pencil and makes a mark on the map. As he reaches to put the rolled-up map back into my tube, I see great tears rolling down his face.

He opens the door and throws me into the air.

****

What a surprise to be flying again! Evening is fast approaching and I circle the cottage to get my bearings. Which way is home? I close my eyes for a few seconds to let my internal compass set itself in the direction of my home. At first, I can't feel it. A tree branch beckons and I drop onto it for a pause, hoping to re-orient the pull I usually feel for my nesting box. Home feels out of reach.

Then, like a tiny sound, I hear and feel the direction I should take. It's a quiet pulsing noise, almost like a heart beating. But it's there, far away to the northwest. Stronger than any of my thoughts, it calls to me and I know I must follow that familiar beating.

I take off. I'm going home.

But first, since this is going to be a long flight and most of it will be over the waters of the English Channel, I think I'd better eat something, roost for the night and set off over the water tomorrow.

I scan the fields below, looking for grain. Sadly, it's late in the summer and most of the harvest has been completed. I'd better find a forest where there might be some late berries. I can find insects while in flight. They're easy to snatch if I fly close to the ground.

However, I am crossing enemy territory. Flying close to the ground might attract the attention of the Germans! The woods it is then! That will be the safest place for me. I spot some trees, just visible on the horizon. I set off.

As I approach, I hear a terrific explosion. The tree line along the edge of the forest seems to burst open, setting free the strangest sort of airplane I've ever seen. It flies low to the ground. The body is sleek and slim. It doesn't appear to have any sort of engine or propellers.

Could this be the Doodlebug? The deadly Nazi un-manned missile used to kill innocent civilians? And its launch site is hidden deep in the forest? How can that be?

Curiosity takes hold of me and before I can think it through, I'm swooping over to have a look.

From above, nothing is visible. I enter the woods under the tree tops and drop to a branch. There is no sign of birds, no rustling noises of animals who normally live here. It's as if the forest has died, no sign of life except for men in strange clothing. My curiosity says: 'Go get a better look'.

Flitting along under the canopy of leaves, I find a perch close enough to observe several men washing down an elevated track with push brooms and buckets of water. They are busy enough not to notice me.

I hear one heavily mustachioed man, dressed in a uniform with SS insignia on his collar, speaking in an unkind way to those working. He's throwing his arms around in rough gestures to punctuate his shouted orders. Clearly, he isn't a pleasant fellow. The workers bend their heads and work faster. That is, all but one, who lifts his chin and says just a few quiet words to the uniformed officer. Even I can see that this is not a good idea. The SS officer already seems angry.

Sure enough, the officer takes two quick steps forward and plunges a fist into the belly of the man who spoke. The worker crumples to the ground.

I am outraged. And just what does a distraught pigeon do?

You guessed right! Taking off from my concealed perch, I swoop low over the SS officer dropping the only bomb I can, directly on his shoulder, spattering the SS patches on his tight collar, as well as all over his ear.

Caught off guard, the officer shakes his head and looks to the sky. I have flown away and stop to perch because I am laughing so hard.

The officer realizes what I have done and spots me. His left hand reaches to his waist and unsnaps a flap. In one smooth gesture, his right hand pulls out a pistol and raises it to take aim. As I'm laughing, the bullet whizzes by my head, blasting leaves and bark from the tree.

High time to get hold of myself before my mission comes to a hasty end, right here and right now! I don't want to be roasted for this SS officer's dinner! Crazed images of his mustache approaching my leg flit through my brain as I burst into flight, followed by a series of bullets trying to stop my escape.

"HALT!!!" he shouts in a furious German voice. As if I'd pay attention to his orders! Silly man, thinking he can control the birds and the bees! He continues to shoot in my general direction, but I veer off through the trees, using their camouflage to hide my escape route.

I feel sorry for the workers left behind because I know the officer is going to be even angrier now, than he was before I'd pooped on his SS badges. But, I also know that sometimes, it's the small things which brighten a tough situation, making it possible to keep going. Hopefully, when the workers are alone at the end of the day, they can have a good laugh. That might bring them perseverance.

In the meantime, I need to look for food. Luckily, I'm still in the woods. There are bugs everywhere and even a few blackberries. On the forest floor, I flip leaves left and right, filling up on insects hiding in the leaf mold.

By now, the sun is gone and I must sleep. Settling in the high branches, far from men and tree climbing cats, I fold my wings and bend my legs to lower my body to the wide branch, relaxed and exhausted from the day's events.

Thoughts whiz through my mind, but most importantly, in the quiet I can feel the pulsing call for home. It's stronger now that the day is ending and quiet is gently falling through the trees in the forest.

'Tomorrow! I'll get back tomorrow,' I say as I close my eyes.

****

It's the dawn chorus of songbirds which wakes me. That, and the unpleasant noise of my growling stomach. Time for a good breakfast, before taking off for the coastline, feeling my nest call to me across the water.

It's easy flying this morning and I soon forget to worry about the possible perils of the long trip ahead of me. I play in the gentle breeze, rising and dipping above the golden stubble of harvested fields. Catching a bug here and there, I'm making nice progress towards the beach.

Ahead are the high cliffs bordering the English Channel, pulling gusts of wind off the water and tossing me high into the air. Gulls wheel and turn, rising on the swirling currents. Swerving among them, I join in their games, adding my song to their screeching calls. We turn and spin around each other, veering in wide arcs on the up-sweep in front of tall chalk cliffs. I'm glad not to be one of them, although I enjoy the feel of these air currents they play in all day. While the gulls are strong and beautifully white, their voices are rather unpleasant. My soft cooing is lost in their noisy squawks. I wonder why they're yelling at each other all the time. Maybe their song has developed in such a way as to be able to hear each other over the crashing waves and whistling winds.

That's enough playing for now. I'll need a good rest before starting across the English Channel. I'll need somewhere quiet to nap and prepare for the long ocean voyage.

I find a roost in a pine tree, bending inland as if pushing away from the sea above the town of Dieppe.

It sits in the front garden of a large house facing the water. The house has been damaged. Broken panes in the windows look out over the water, as if shouting for help across the Channel to England. The roof is partly gone and I can see the gaily papered bedroom of children who used to live here. I wonder where they have gone?

Suddenly, I hear voices speaking in German. They are very close to me. The tree I have perched in sits just next to a little hill. A hidden stairway reaches underground through tall grass and two German soldiers are climbing the stairs just beneath me. I sit very still, hoping they won't lift their heads. If they see me, I am as good as cooked. One cautious side step at a time, I begin to move closer to the trunk of the pine, hoping to hide next to it until they leave.

Good grief, they're having a cigarette and a chat! How long before one of them lifts his gaze and notices me here? The other night, Joseph explained that all the pigeons in France have been eaten by the occupying army. Carrier pigeons, such as myself, are strictly forbidden.

I glance down at the tube attached to my leg, realizing it's bright red. Why, oh why does it have to be red? A nice leafy green color would have been so much smarter! But, no, it's very red! You'd think the person who thought that was a good idea wants us to be shot by German soldiers! And to think humans make unkind remarks about bird brains!

Another sliding step towards the tree trunk when they're not looking. Maybe I can slip away to the cover of the branches and disappear from their line of vision. Another side-step...almost there...

Out of nowhere, one of the gulls makes a sloppy landing right next to me, cawing loudly and shaking the branch so that pine cones fall around the Germans. The gull turns to me and squawks a greeting as the soldiers look up, squinting through the branches.

Of course, as they see the bright red tube on my leg, their unfinished cigarettes fall from their open mouths and they begin to shout and raise their guns, aiming in my direction.

I'm off through the branches, fighting the powerful currents of wind sweeping over the top of the cliffs, I'm stuck flapping in the same spot as the winds push against my body. Bullets whizz by me to the left and to the right. I have no choice but to fold my wings in and dive straight down the front of the cliff.

Plunging down, I'm headed for a crash landing on the rocks below unless I can unfold my wings and take off across the waves. I try to pull my shoulder muscles out to unfold, but the air currents I'm diving through are too strong! I'm gaining too much speed! The rocks are getting closer and closer until finally, one wing unfolds and I feel a snap as I veer off, slowing into a spin. The other wing opens and I can fly straight, skimming just above the surface of the waves.

I'm safe from the German soldiers, but now I have a long journey across open water with nowhere to land for a rest. I close my eyes and focus on the beating call of home, adjust my flight path slightly and get going.

****

Hours pass and I see no sign of land. I can still feel the pulsing signal of home. So, I concentrate on that. I cannot let myself feel tired.

I try not to think about food. I try not to think about anything but the happy, colorful wallpaper on the child's bedroom walls behind the broken windows of that house I left behind on the coast of France.

I think about the tears on Emile's face just before he threw me into the air. I think about the SS officer and his mustache. I think about the sad looking men, too frightened to speak up to him. I think about the one who did and the

pain he felt as he fell to the ground.

I think about Joseph and the stories he told of his dangerous journey. I think that I must keep flapping my wings and keep thinking. Perseverance.

Night comes and still no sign of lights along a coastline. I've never flown in the dark. We're in bed by nightfall. I'm frightened. I hear noises of waves and wind, like in the daylight but they seem louder and scarier when I can't see where I'm going. There are clouds blocking the light of the moon and I feel drops of rain carried on the wind. I try closing my eyes in case that's easier than looking for something in the dark that isn't there.

Suddenly, I hear a low rumbling in the distance. A flash lights the horizon as a bolt of lightning strikes the water. I can see for a brief second. I've never flown in a thunderstorm, either. The raindrops are heavier and strike my wings and body like tiny rocks. They hurt. The wind is pushing against me, slowing me down and making it harder to fly. But, I must keep flapping my wings, because I've nowhere to land. I cannot land on the surface of the water like gulls or ducks. My feathers are not water proof! I'll sink! But this rain hurts! And I'm so very tired. And scared. And so alone.

I want to give up. I cannot continue. I can't see any way that I can succeed. I have to stop flying. I'll fall into the water. I'll die. I am so tired. Maybe it's better if I just quit. I close my eyes again and slow my flapping. My body feels so heavy. Exhausted, I begin to descend toward the surface of the water.

Just above the water, I hear a loud, metallic clicking sound. I open my eyes as a huge, silvery shape flies just above me. The rush of wind as it passes over me, lifts me away from the surface of the water and pulls me along faster and faster as I'm sucked into the massive drag of air behind it.

It's one of the V1 missiles headed towards England!

I'm wide awake now and still being pulled by the wind behind the V1 which is now far ahead of me. The drag slows, but I'm feeling much more alert.

'Just keeping flapping your wings!' I tell myself, 'Perseverance, or stubborn pigeon brain!' Whichever keeps me going. I shout at myself like my clumsy friends the gulls. 'Keep going, Zip! You can do this! Innocent civilians need you to bring this map back to England! Emile trusted you to carry this message! Now do it.'

Another blaze of light bursts on the horizon, but this time I know it isn't lightning. It's the V1 which has exploded. I can see the light from the fire it has caused. The missile has crashed on the top of a cliff. Fire and smoke shoot up into the sky.

But wait! It's on the top of a cliff! That means I've made it across the water! I'll be able to land soon! Just a few more miles! Just a little more perseverance! I think of the fire and smoke on the top of the cliff and remember why I've made this journey. I must get home with my message so that the Allied bombers can put a stop to these deadly missiles crashing into coastlines and harming innocent people.

'Just keep flapping your wings, Zip!' I shout at myself as if I were a gull screaming into the wind.

The smell of burning grass hits me in the face as I approach the coastline. The upsweep of air lifts me over the top of the white chalk cliffs and I stretch my legs in front of me for the first time in hours as I drop to the ground. I must find somewhere to rest, eat something, then get airborne again because the map in my tube must be delivered.

But just for a few minutes, how wonderful it feels to walk! I strut around in the grass for the fun of it, just because I can. I'm enjoying myself, stalking through the grass and catching bugs for just a short break when I feel the pulsing call from my nesting box reach out to me. Time to get going again!

Dawn is breaking as I see the tall chimneys and peaked rooflines of Bletchley Park reaching up through the trees, guiding me home.

Feeling like I've been brought back from the dead, I zoom above the yard, circling until one of the handlers notices me and shouts. I'm waiting for several of them to gather as they run across the yard from different directions. I can hear the rustling and shuffling of pigeon feet in the straw of the nesting boxes. Finally, I hear my mother's coo.

"Zip? My darling boy, is that you?" she calls.

"Zip! Tell us it's you! You've made it back!" shouts Horatio.

As I land, more and more coos reach me above the excited talking of the handlers as I'm carried off into a building to deliver the precious map in my bright red tube.

My heart beats warmly, pleased to be home, anxious to greet those I love, excited to tell my story and satisfied to have completed my first mission.

****

We are ushered into a large room with important looking men gathered around a table. Large maps are pinned to the wall.

"Well, is this the young fellow just back from France?" asks a uniformed man.

"Yes, Sir! This is the one." My handler is beaming with pride.

"Stubborn little fellow, isn't he?" says the Officer, as he strokes the feathers on my head.

"No, Sir. He's learned the meaning of the word perseverance, Sir. He's learned when it's a good thing to put your mind to something and to be stubborn about it."

Tails of War

"Zip: The Story of a Carrier Pigeon in WWII" is inspired by the numerous animal recipients of the Dickin Medal of Honor for outstanding loyalty and service during times of war. Founded during the Second World War by Maria Dickin, the medal has been awarded to 4 horses, 28 dogs, 32 pigeons and a single cat.

Zip's character is a composite of the adventures of many of those pigeons. Since this book is a work of fiction, I've taken the liberty of giving Zip a say in what might have happened to those pigeons during their missions, as the men who handled them could never know.

I learned about the many roles of carrier pigeons in WW2 a long time ago while doing research for my first historical fiction novel for adults: "Through These Doors". Some alert readers will remember a familiar scene from that book, this time told from the point of view of the pigeon.

The museums at Pegasus Bridge and at Utah Beach contributed to my research by providing a close up look at the pigeon transportation cages and images of award ceremonies involving brave birds. The Val Ygot Association in Normandy hosts an open-air museum giving visitors a look at a real V1 launch site and a Doodlebug missile. The church at Auppegard contains a stained-glass window and a monument to the civilians who lost their lives on June 16th, 1944 in a horrific accident, while the Nazis nearby were testing the range of their deadly weapon.

I may be repeating myself, but I hope that those who read this story may be inspired to learn more about HISTORY.

47567328R00038

Made in the USA
Middletown, DE
28 August 2017